For Louie, our rescued dog—
H.Z.

Published in the United States 2012 by
Blue Apple Books, 515 Valley Street,
Maplewood, NJ 07040
www.blueapplebooks.com
First Edition
Printed in China 04/12
ISBN: 978-1-60905-187-7
1 3 5 7 9 10 8 6 4 2

Harriet Ziefert

LUCY
RESCUED

Paintings by Barroux

BLUE 🍎 APPLE

Here is Lucy at the pound,
where we found her.

She needed to be rescued.
Her time was almost up.

We filled out adoption papers
and brought her home.

I showed Lucy around the house.

Then I showed her our yard.

Lucy heard the neighbor's dog barking.
She hid under a bush and
would not come out . . .

even when I held out dog yummies.

I finally got Lucy to come out
from behind the bush.
I carried her to my room.

WAH-OOO-OOO
WAH-OOO-OOO
WAH-OOO-OOO
WAH-OOO-OOO
WAH-OOO-OOO
WAH-OOO-OOO
WAH-OOO
WAH-OOO
WAH-OOO-OOO

That's when the howling began.

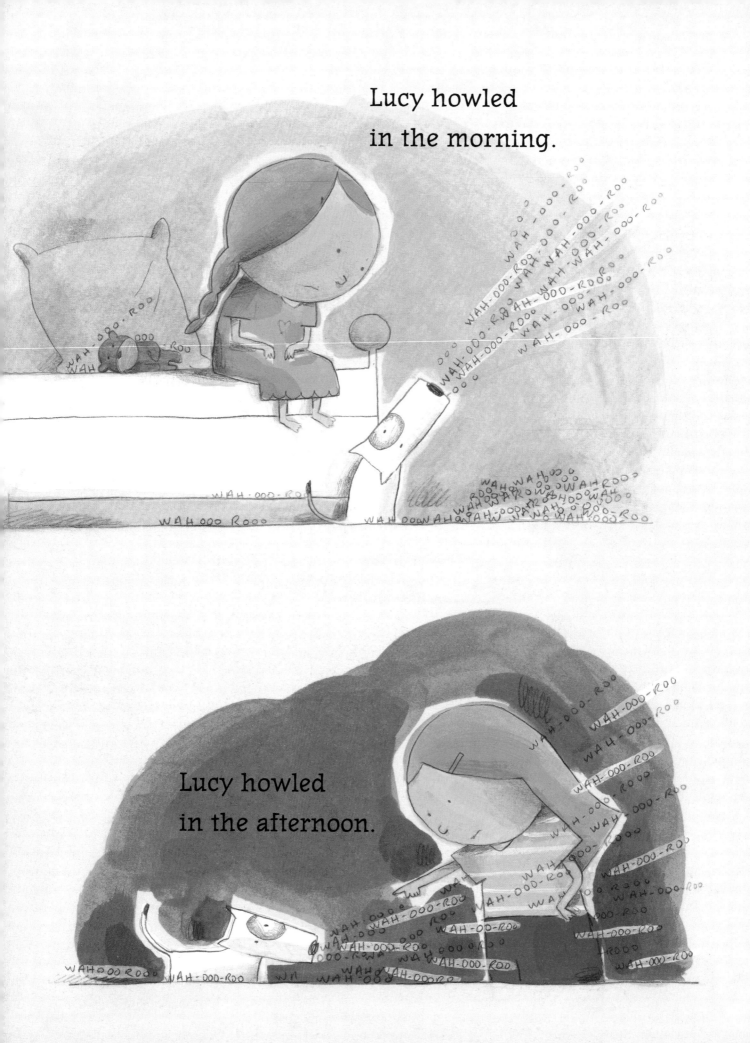

By the time evening came,
the howling was so loud
I put on earmuffs.

Dad thought our new dog was lonely for other dogs, so he brought her a mirror.

Lucy cried to the dog in the mirror.

Mom cooked Lucy a special meal.
And I offered her treats.

But food didn't stop the howling.

Then I had an idea.

"Maybe Lucy needs a new bed?"

Mom bought a nice, soft, comfy one.

"WAH-OOO-OOO-ROO!"

cried Lucy.

Dad took Lucy to a dog psychologist.
His specialty was nervous dogs.
The doctor spent an hour talking to Lucy
and doing tests.

Then he talked to Dad.
"Play classical music," he said. "Or lullabies.
Or singers singing sweet songs."

We played the soft music.
Lucy howled along.

"WAH-OOO-OOO-ROO!"

Mom said,
"Lucy's just not happy here.
Let's try for one more night.
If Lucy does not settle down,
we'll have to return her
to the pound."

I had one last idea.
"Lucy, I think you need a friend."

I gave her my
favorite stuffed animal.

WAH-OOO-ROO
WAH-OOO-ROO
WAH-OOO-ROO
WAH-OOO-ROO
WAH-OOO-ROO
WAH-OOO-ROO
WAH-OOO-ROO
WAH-OOO-ROO
WAH-OOO-ROO
WAH-OOO-ROO
WAH-OOO-ROO
WAH-OOO-ROO
WAH-OOO-ROO
WAH-OOO-ROO
WAH-OOO-ROO
WAH-OOO-ROO

Lucy snuggled with my toy.
The howling stopped, and
we all slept really well.

In the morning, Lucy jumped on my bed
and grabbed another one of my toys.

"That's not yours!" I yelled. "It's mine!"

Lucy held MY toy in her mouth
and would not give it up!

During the day, Lucy moved her two
new friends all around the house
and played doggie games with them.

I gave Lucy a few of my not-so-favorite
animals to add to her collection.

Mom and Dad bought Lucy more toys.
Right now, Lucy has four dogs, two bears,
two kittens, and one giraffe.

Before going to sleep at night, Lucy collects all
of her furry friends and puts them in her soft bed.

When one is missing, she searches all over for it.

"You'll find it tomorrow," I say.

But Lucy just says,

"WAH-OOO-OOO-ROO!"

"Okay! Okay! I'll help you!" I tell her.

I look downstairs . . .

upstairs . . .

but I can't find
her toy anywhere.

I climb into bed, hoping that Lucy
will forget about her missing toy.
But she does not.

Soon I feel Lucy tugging
on my blue blanket.

"Lucy, you found your giraffe!
Now we can go to bed!"

"Good night,
my perfect
puppy!"